Henry Holt and Company, *Publishers since 1866*

Henry Holt® is a registered trademark of Macmillan Publishing Group, LLC

120 Broadway, New York, NY 10271 · mackids.com

Library of Congress Cataloging-in-Publication Data is available.

Our books may be purchased in bulk for promotional, educational, or business use.

Please contact your local bookseller or the Macmillan Corporate and Premium Sales Department

at (800) 221-7945 ext. 5442 or by email at MacmillanSpecialMarkets@macmillan.com.

The illustrations for this book were created with ink pens, watercolor, and colored pencils.

Printed in China by Hung Hing Off-set Printing Co. Ltd., Heshan City, Guangdong Province

ISBN 978-1-250-82273-4

1 3 5 7 9 10 8 6 4 2

LORNA SCOBIE

DUCK, DUCK, DAD?

HENRY HOLT AND COMPANY

New York

Ralph enjoyed a quiet life.
He liked going on quiet walks to smell
the flowers, past the butterflies and trees,
past . . .

. . . an egg?

CRACK!

Ralph wasn't sure that he wanted a duckling.

But the duckling wanted him.

Dad?

It didn't seem very quiet. **Dad?**

But at least it was just the one.

Dad!

Ralph wasn't at all sure how to look after his new ducklings.

They **definitely** weren't quiet.

But he decided to try.

They needed things all the time.

Did ducklings eat . . .
Dog food?
Broccoli?

Bath time was actually rather fun . . .

. . . most of the time.

With a little help from the ducklings, Ralph mastered the doggy paddle.

And Ralph got bedtime cuddles just right.

Sometimes it was lovely and quiet . . .

... but just for a while.

Is it MORNING NOW, Dad?

We are AWAKE, Dad!

Can I have breakfast please?

Ralph was almost beginning to enjoy his new noisy life.

Things were going very well . . .

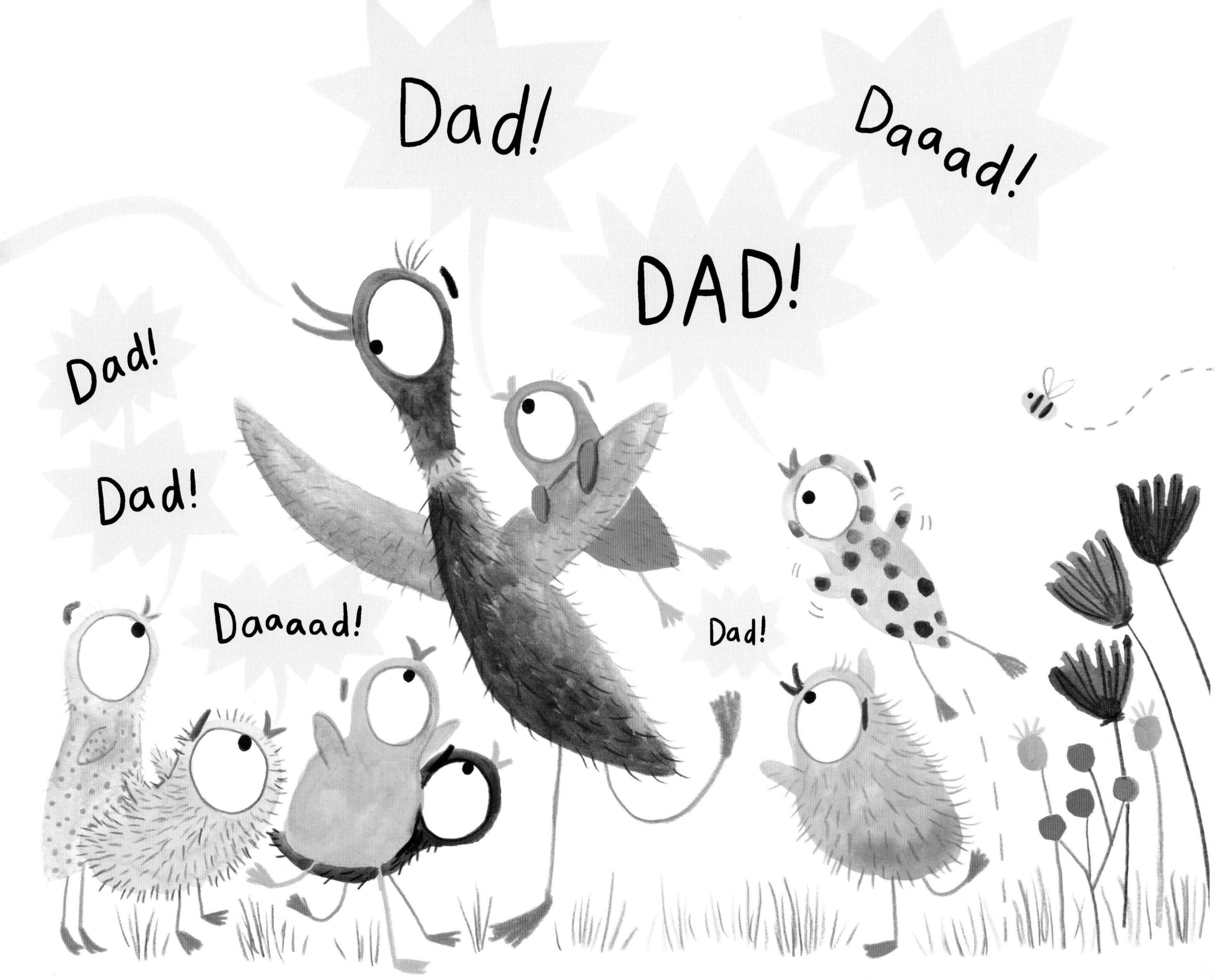
Dad!
Daaad!
DAD!
Dad!
Dad!
Daaaad!
Dad!

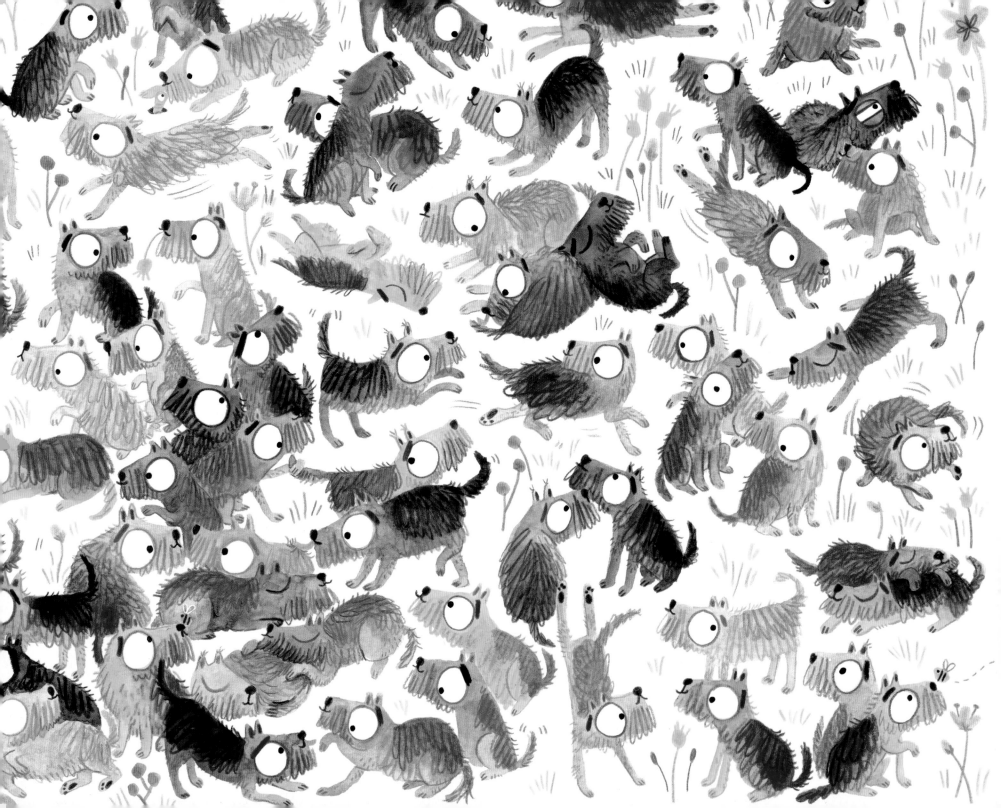

Ralph loved his new puppies.

Dad, please can we dig for bones?

Please can we have a story?

A long one please!

Please can you race us?

But he also loved his ducklings.

So they decided to become one BIG family!

It wasn't the quiet life for Ralph anymore . . .

But it was full of CUDDLES!